THIS BOOK BELONGS TO:

_____

_____

THE BLACK AND WHITE CLUB

Written by Alice Hemming

Illustrated by Kimberley Scott

For Simon

George was enjoying a quiet evening in the Heavenly Hippos Wildlife Park. Suddenly he spotted a group of animals creeping past.

He stopped his best friend Seymour to find out where they were going.

"To the Black and White Club, " said Seymour. "The penguins invited us…They have dominoes!"

"Sounds exciting!" said George. "Can I join?"

"Better ask the penguins," said Seymour.

"You have to be black and white. Or black. Or white."

"Sorry!" called Seymour as he went in without George.

The following night, George tried to sneak in
the back way, but it didn't work.

The night after that, he went in disguise.
That didn't work either.

George decided he would make his own club - the Giraffes Only Club.

He then remembered he was the only giraffe at the Wildlife Park.

So he started the Yellow with Brown Spots Club.
It only had two members but it did give him an idea...

Soon the Tall and Short Club was formed. They prepared for the very first meeting.

They wrote a list of rules and regulations, and printed off some special badges.

Their new club attracted lots of members.

THE TALL AND SHORT CLUB

"Can I join?" asked Toni.
"Yes!" said George.

"Can I join?" asked Minnie.
"Yes!" said George.

"Can I join?" asked Gus.
George wasn't sure. Gus didn't look tall or short.

"I'm tall this way," he said, stretching out his arms.
"Ok, then!" said George.

"I'm taller than him," said Mo.

"And I'm shorter than her," said Max.
"Ok, then!" said George.

"Can I be in two clubs at once?"
asked Seymour.
"Of course!" said George, who
could not have been happier.

Soon, all the animals at the park had joined, even the black and white ones. Except the penguins…

...They stuck to playing dominoes.

The End

The Black and White Club
An original concept by author Alice Hemming
© Alice Hemming

Illustrated by Kimberley Scott
Represented by Advocate Art

Published by MAVERICK ARTS PUBLISHING LTD

3A Horsham City Business Centre
Brighton Road, Horsham, West Sussex, RH13 5BB
© Maverick Arts Publishing Limited September 2013 +44 (0) 1403 256941

A CIP catalogue record for this book is available at the British Library

ISBN 978-1-84886-096-4

Maverick
arts publishing
www.maverickbooks.co.uk

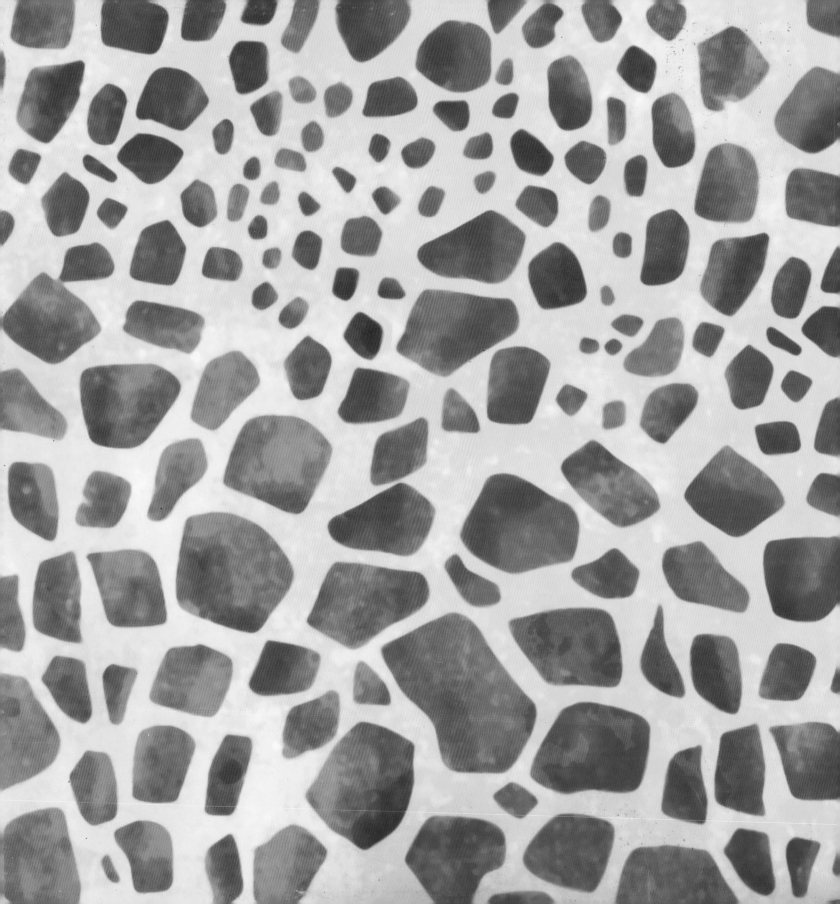